I0624308

Milton
Marmalade's
Remarkably
Silly Stories for
Grown-ups

Narrow Gate Press
London MMXVIII

Dedicated to everyone with a curly mind

Published by Narrow Gate Press,
BM Box 6798
London
WC1N 3XX

www.ngp.co
info@ngp.co
www.MiltonMarmalade.uk

All characters are fictitious unless they obviously aren't, in which case I shall head the relevant story with an appropriate disclaimer.

Cover design and illustrations: Martin Dace

Copyright © 2018 Milton Marmalade & Martin Dace

Diving into the Library previously published in Sharon Gordon, *Treasured Chests*, 2011.

Set in IM Fell. The Fell Types are digitally reproduced by Igino Marini www.iginomarini.com

ISBN 978-0-9565497-7-8

Thema classification: FU (Humorous fiction)
BIC classification: FYB (Short stories), DCF (Poetry)

A dire warning

Remarkably Silly Stories and poems are all copyright, all rights reserved, and if you steal my stories and I later get famous my lawyers will certainly be after you.

My lawyers are called Bloodfang & Wolf and they have a reputation. If you go into their office on a full moon you will find yourself at the front desk where a very pretty woman sits.

In one corner is a carved wooden candlestick holding a fat off-white church candle, its tiny flame guttering ineffectually.

You see the woman by the moonlight streaming through the gothic windows. She is wearing a black dress calculated to show off her figure, in which roundness in all the right places is emphasised by an almost unfeasably small waist. She has raven hair and her eyes are pools of darkness. Though she is beautiful you feel for a moment as though you are staring into the soul of an animal.

You ask to see one of the partners but she tells you ever so sweetly that since it is a full moon neither of them are in. However she assures you that your case is in the best hands and anyone who steals your work will be sure to regret it.

Somewhere outside you hear a scream which you think may be a fox or maybe not. Because she is smiling at you, and also because her low cut dress suggests breasts of surpassing wonder, you think about asking her out on a date. The moonlight casts a glint on one of her unusually sharp canine teeth.

You lose your nerve and find yourself out on the pavement again wondering quite what happened. The fox, or whatever it was, screams again, briefly, then there is silence.

Contents

The girl who was not a vampire

Myrtle had freckles, huge glasses with pebble lenses, and a terrible secret. She was also hopelessly infatuated with the bad boy of the class, Zigmond Bloodfang.

Actually most of the boys in the class were bad, except Freddy Märchen. Freddy was sweet-natured and had a loving heart, which is why the other boys used to set on him in the boys' toilet, push his head into the toilet bowl and pull the chain.

As for Zigmond, or Ziggy to his friends, he was the worst bad boy and he barely deigned to notice Myrtle's existence. Unlike some of the bad boys, he didn't wear a wide silk cravat round his neck. This might turn out to be a significant plot detail, then again, it might not.

Ziggy had a nonchalant grin that was calculated to send a frisson through any girl, starting with her toes and travelling towards her head via various other anatomical sites en route. He used it on Cynthia Moonbreath and she got the frisson right in the pit of her stomach. A less steely-hearted girl would have imagined she was in love. Since Cynthia was beautiful and knew it, she did not fall in love, but merely dived into her desk for an antacid tablet which she kept there for just such eventualities. On emerging again she flicked her raven hair behind her strangely luminous face and smiled at him ambiguously. Ziggy's grin faded because he knew he wasn't the boss any more.

"I want you to beg me," he thought.

"I know you want me to beg you," she thought. "Too bad."

Myrtle looked on in anguish, wanting him so badly. Clearly to attract a boy you have to be nonchalant like that, and then ambiguous.

"Or if not him then I would settle for one of the other bad boys," she thought, "or in fact any boy, except Freddy, who is not a bad boy at all." What was it about bad boys that made them attractive?

"What should I do?" Myrtle asked her best friend Felicity. Felicity was black and comely, as it says in the Good Book (Song of Solomon 1:5). She loved Myrtle for who she was, neither because of nor despite her freckles and pebble lenses.

"Boys like a challenge," Felicity said. "You have to be nonchalant and then ambiguous."

Myrtle tried being nonchalant for several days and Ziggy didn't notice her at all, so she never got to the ambiguous part.

In the corridor on the way to maths class Freddy asked her about the diagonal in a square homework question, but she was so busy being nonchalant that she just said, "Square root of two." She didn't see his eyes full of wonder. Felicity saw Freddy's eyes full of wonder, but she thought it was because he was awed by Myrtle's grasp of surds.[*]

"Did you see Freddy's eyes full of wonder?" she asked Myrtle.

"Freddy is sweet," was all Myrtle replied.

'But what was Myrtle's terrible secret?' I hear you ask. As it happens Felicity was to find it out the very next day.

"You know of course that every young teenager is either a vampire or a werewolf these days?" Myrtle said.

Felicity nodded in apparent agreement, her lips pursed. It was a sunny day and they were sitting on the lawn at the back of the school, out of earshot of anyone else. In the distance two figures were in a furtive embrace, and a keen eye might have thought it was Cynthia and Ziggy. A keener eye might have seen Cynthia love-biting Ziggy's neck in a reversal of the time-honoured vampire tradition, and Ziggy looking pale with two streaks of blood running down from Cynthia's kiss.

---

[*] Surds: you know, those square root thingys.

Let us not dwell on the question of whether Ziggy was a virgin, nor speculate on what might happen to Cynthia if he wasn't. There was a school sick room and we shall leave all that unpleasantness to the school nurse to sort out if the occasion arises. She is paid to do that.

"Well..." Myrtle faltered.

Felicity looked with a mixture of anxiety and hope at Myrtle, not daring to guess what Myrtle might say next, because in her heart she sensed something of what it might be. Myrtle turned to make eye-contact with her friend and held both of Felicity's hands.

"Promise never to tell?"

"I promise." Felicity did not blink. Myrtle squeezed her hands.

"I... I'm not a vampire and I'm not a werewolf." She stopped, scanning her friend's face for a reaction.

Felicity said nothing at first. There was a moment's hesitation then she flung her arms around her friend's neck and hugged her. With her mouth close to Myrtle's ear she whispered, "I'm not a vampire or a werewolf either. I'm actually a wood-nymph. Don't tell anyone."

Myrtle pulled back, her eyes wide. "No, I mean, I'm not anything. I'm not even a dryad. I'm not magic at all."

Felicity recoiled. How could such a thing happen? How could a girl who was not magic in any way have got into school undetected, living all this time unsuspected among teenage vampires and werewolves?

There had always been talk of some dark secret in Nosferatu Academy, something or someone who did not belong and whose presence threatened everything the Academy stood for. Could it be that behind Myrtle's strange appearance lurked a being horribly, insatiably normal?

"Perhaps you are a mermaid?" Felicity suggested. "I know you are very shy about being seen in the shower after games."

"Not even that." Myrtle spoke in a barely audible whisper.

Now Felicity knew the truth. An ordinary person in their midst, and it was her own best friend. She turned her head away and started to gag, at first uncontrollably, but with an effort mastered herself and turned back to face Myrtle, her face a strange colour. "You..." she faltered.

"I... I can't help being me!" Myrtle cried, rivers of tears coursing down her cheeks. "I didn't choose not to be magic!" She buried her face in her hands and sat motionless, occasional sobs shaking her body.

Felicity sat there, stunned, for what seemed an hour but must have been less. Somewhere a long way off a cry was heard, and a girl could be seen running from the bushes clutching her neck. Then emerged a girl with a luminous face and raven hair sauntering across the lawn with a strange smile playing about her lips, which seemed unusually red. Cynthia could accomplish a lot in one break-time.

At last Felicity's hand stretched towards Myrtle and tentatively touched Myrtle's shoulder.

"We've always been friends," she said. "Perhaps... perhaps something can be done. I could take you to Dr Frankenstein. He might be able to help."

Myrtle looked up and saw Felicity's face through a haze of tears. "No," she said emphatically. "Accept me as I am, or go away."

Felicity said nothing. Perhaps she understood what it was to be the odd one out. After all, most vampires are pale and she was accepted only on sufferance. What might happen if they found out she was only a wood-nymph she dreaded to think.

The bell went and the girls stood up. As they walked back to class, Felicity reached out for Myrtle's hand and held it. There ahead of them was Freddy. He turned and smiled at Myrtle. For the first time she didn't inwardly recoil. Freddy was sweet, not exciting like the other boys. But there was one thing special about him, and that was that he smiled at her, today. Somehow that mattered, right now. She didn't even care that his hair was wet.

"Square root of two," Freddy said. "I like surds, don't you?"

"Not really," Myrtle replied, and then wished she'd said something else. Freddy blushed, turned and walked on, gazing at the floor.

As they entered the classroom Myrtle could see Ziggy sitting at his desk, tilting his chair on its back legs and trying to look cool. But there was something lacking. His grin was more forced and he looked pale. His eyes looked empty. And unlike earlier in the day a wide silk cravat concealed his neck.

Even in her state of anguish Myrtle noticed this detail. She looked around and saw that quite a lot of the boys and some of the girls wore silk scarves too. More than she remembered. But not Freddy. Cynthia turned to smile at Freddy, who looked confused but tried to smile back. Cynthia continued to stare at him and locked her gaze into his. Then she pointed to him and back to herself, slowly and deliberately. "After school," she mouthed.

"Cynthia is running out of victims," Felicity whispered into Myrtle's ear. If it was possible for Myrtle's face to look more anguished than before, it did.

All eyes were to the front as Dr Finsternis rapped his knuckles on the teacher's desk for the start of the lesson on the construction of pentagrams for nefarious purposes. "The theoretical appreciation of pentagrams involves surds," he said. "You all know how much you enjoy surds." And he gave an amused grimace as the class groaned.

After class Freddy was first to leave since his desk was nearest the door, and Myrtle and Felicity got stuck behind a crowd of other students all pushing and shoving. That's what happens if you are not a naturally pushy person. Somewhere in the middle of the crowd was Cynthia, looking serene in a disturbing way as was her wont. She would certainly make it through the door before they did.

Myrtle grabbed Felicity's wrist. "What shall we do?" she asked. Felicity needed no further explanation, and she pulled Myrtle into the crowd, pushing forward as best as she could. However it made no difference in this bestial melee and they were the last to leave the classroom. Cynthia was a long way ahead of them, almost floating down the corridor as if in no hurry, and Freddy was nowhere to be seen.

They ran on. Somehow, although Cynthia did not run, it was impossible to catch up with her. Myrtle felt as if she were in one of those dreams in which your legs seem to move but you cannot run, and whatever fate is about to engulf you gets closer and closer until you wake up. There was something not quite right going on, something a wood-nymph's magic was insufficient to deal with.

Felicity turned and dragged Myrtle with her. "Round the back!" she hissed. The two friends ran back down the corridor, out through the little gap in the gothic stonework and into the herb garden, making a short cut through mandrakes, henbane and black hellebores. Here was where the school kept its garden of venomous vegetables. Over in the corner weeds had established themselves too - a clump of tall stems with little globes of white flowers that exploded like fireworks. Someone had been in there and picked a few. Then on through the back entrance to the alchemy laboratory, past luminous blue retorts and bubbling amber liquids and out the other side. Panting in the doorway, they could see the tall clipped hedges that formed the school's maze of yew battlements, places where moonstruck girls had sometimes been hunted by werewolves. The sun was setting and the place was falling into twilight. There, glimpsed somewhere behind a leafy wall were two figures in a topiary arch. One was tall with raven hair framing a luminous face with bright red lips, and the other was shorter, a boy. The boy was holding a bunch of flowers - tall stems with little globes of white flowers that exploded like fireworks. The girl was bending towards the boy's neck.

"Freddy!" Myrtle shouted.

At first nothing happened. The girl's face hovered next to Freddy's neck unmoving. Then slowly she straightened up and turned towards where Myrtle's voice had come from. The boy hardly moved at all. Then the girl walked away and disappeared somewhere inside the maze. In the distance they heard a strangled gurgling sound like someone being sick.

"Freddy!" Myrtle half cried, half sobbed.

Freddy turned and smiled. He made his way through paths this way and that until he was once again outside the maze. Slowly he walked towards the two friends. Myrtle smiled a little too, then her smile disappeared. Freddy's neck was concealed under a silk cravat.

Still smiling, although now with a tinge of worry, Freddy handed the flowers to Myrtle. "For you," he said, a little doubtfully. Myrtle took them, her face a blank. The flowers had a kind of jubilant beauty, she thought distractedly. She gave one to Felicity to look at. Freddy stood there like a statue, not sure what to do next.

How long they would have stood there in silence I do not know. Suddenly Felicity could stand it no longer. "Freddy!" she said, "Why are you wearing a cravat?"

"Oh that!" Freddy said. "I knew Cynthia was up to no good so I dug up a piece of garlic from the herb garden and wrapped it in a cravat round my neck. Cynthia hates garlic, you know."

"So... so she didn't bite you?" Myrtle asked.

With that Freddy pulled the cravat from his neck. His neck was unmarked.

"Oh!" Myrtle exclaimed.

"Now I know something about you," Freddy said, and this time his eyes twinkled mischievously.

"What?" Myrtle asked nervously.

He lowered his voice to a whisper. "You are not a vampire. Neither of you are vampires."

"How... how do you know?" both girls talked at once.

"Because you've been holding that bunch of garlic flowers for the last several minutes and neither of you got ill."

"But..." Myrtle began.

"And another thing." Here he faltered. "Myrtle I..." He waited nervously and said nothing more. All the time he gazed into Myrtle's eyes.

It was getting dark and Felicity wanted to go home. "Please get it over with," she said. She went round to Freddy's back and gave him a shove, causing him to fall onto Myrtle, who instinctively grabbed him round the chest. Her glasses steamed up. Gently, Freddy took them off. "You are the most magical person I know," he said.

"I do like surds really," Mytle said, and with that they kissed. Not a bite on the neck with two little dribbles of blood, but a proper kiss, a long kiss with lips.

The heartbreaking breakup of One Direction

"No, you can't have a sick note. I don't do sick notes for schools. Now then, young Chardonnay, One Direction are only breaking up from each other. They're not breaking up from you. Dry your eyes and get a grip. Next please!"

Elegy on the demise of *The Three Compasses**

Forever Friday nights have lost their magic:
A pub in Rotherhithe, once full, now tragic,
Its fortune turned, like Thames' shore at low tide
Lies all exposed, and with a skip outside.
O, late at night long-leggèd girls once strutted
Where now the pub *Three Compasses* lies gutted.

No more on weekend nights the noisy roar
With ev'ry opening of the saloon door,
No more the visitors from far away
From Surrey Quays and darkest Bermondsey,
No more the youths in jeans and loose T-shirt,
The almost-women with more leg than skirt,
No more the 'private' party after closing,
The disco blast and late at night carousing,
The lonely midnight cry against the din,
Shouting, "Oi it's Tracey, let me in!"

---

* This poem records true events, but that was a long time ago. I have no knowledge of the current state of the establishment that now inhabits the site.

Alas! No more the evening cries are heard
Of public theatre of the absurd:
"Kevin, b———d, you're a total kn–b,
"Why don't you f———g go and get a job?"
Tracey undaunted bellows in the street,
Kevin the while is silent in defeat.

At last in groups the young things drift from sight;
Their loud farewells make echo on the night,
And some to distant homes still chattering go
To music of the in-car stereo.
The lights are out and everyone has gone –
The last car door bangs shut at half past one.
This door of paradise, so much frequented,
So often late, it now lies unlamented.

Here the dart-board leans against a wall,
The tacky pictures, carpets brown, and all
The bar, the pumps, the furnishings are gone.
A solitary table, all alone
Rests on the pavement. As a last regret
A lonely woman drags a cigarette.

Chocolatina and the Carob Cake

Chocolatina was a little girl who didn't stand any nonsense. One day her mother Angelika took her into an organic cafe. There were lots of aging hippies there, with wild looking toddlers in buggies. There were a lot of cakes that looked a bit dry but some of them at least had chocolate on top.

"Please may I have one of those?" Chocolatina asked politely, because although she didn't stand any nonsense she saw no reason to cause unnecessary aggravation. Her mother Angelika first ordered two circular things which Japanese people had made out of rice in such a clever way that they looked exactly like puffed polystyrene. "It's macrobiotic," she explained. Then she chose a cake made out of oats for herself and ordered very weak tarragon tea for both of them and she ordered the chocolate topped thing for Chocolatina.

Although Chocolatina was a girl who didn't stand any nonsense, she was more or less used to very weak tarragon tea, and accepted the bad smell that always went with it and the sensation of emptiness in the stomach as a normal part of life. She therefore bore it patiently. Also she looked forward to the chocolate, even if the cake underneath looked like a brick.

Her mother approved of organic things so Chocolatina supposed that the suffering of eating them was worth it because if you ate organic things you would probably live for ever, or at any rate a very long time. Certainly, as Chocolatina sank her teeth into the polystyrene thing even a minute seemed to last hours. She sat staring at the cafe clock as she chewed it. The second hand clicked slowly round as Chocolatina's mouth tried to make the first bite into something that could be swallowed. If you ate these all the time, Chocolatina thought to herself, and every minute seemed like an hour, then if you lived to seventy you would certainly feel as though you were 4,200 years old. (Chocolatina was very good at mental arithmetic. She was brilliant at mental arithmetic actually. But that has nothing to do with the story). Although Chocolatina was a girl who did not stand any nonsense, she didn't approve of spitting things out, because that always looks gross.

Because of the polystyrene, Chocolatina drank an abnormal amount of very weak tarragon tea, in spite of the smell getting right up her nose. At last she was completely full up with the almost nothing at all that she had eaten. She imagined the Japanese polystyrene bits in her stomach, floating around in a sea of slightly tinted warm water. Yes, I shall certainly live a long time, she thought, even though I am very thin. (Her mother could never understand why Chocolatina was so thin, because after all she fed her such a healthy diet.)

Unfortunately there was still about a quarter of the polystyrene thing left on Chocolatina's plate. Her eyes turned towards the cake; at any rate, she looked at the chocolate part. She started to push away the plate with the polystyrene on it.

"No!" said her mother. "You must finish your main course before you have cake, otherwise you won't get the right vitamins."

"But Angelika," Chocolatina said (she called her mother 'Angelika' because this was a modern liberated thing to do), "Angelika, I'm full up."

"Just eat that little bit," Angelika said.

Chocolatina stared at the piece of polystyrene, which seemed larger than when she had started. "But I'm not hungry any more," she said.

"If you're not hungry for main course then you're not hungry for cake," Angelika said.

Now every child knows this is not true, but no child so far in the history of the world has been able to explain why. Here is the reason. Every child has two stomachs: a main course stomach and a pudding stomach. It works like this: if you eat sweets or pudding first, then the sweets go to your main stomach and your main course can't get in until after the sweets have gone, which is usually after the meal has been cleared away. If you complain about it you are told it's your own fault and why didn't you eat when there was food on the table? You have to wait until the next meal, which is hours.

If, on the other hand, you eat your main course first as your mother tells you, then your pudding stomach is still empty. Now there is no way you can get those last three green beans (let alone a lump of polystyrene) into your main course stomach when it is full up, and green beans and polystyrene absolutely refuse to go in your pudding stomach. Your pudding stomach is a special place and no green beans are allowed in.

It is certain that if you do eat those last three green beans they will make you feel ill, and if you do it too often then when you are grown up you will never know when to stop eating because you always forced too much food into your main course stomach when you were a child. Listen to your stomach. It knows better than your mother when it is full up.

But cake is another matter. Cake slips right round all the green beans and on into the pudding stomach, easy as anything.

In the future scientists will prove, sure as sure, that cake, especially sticky cake, and especially especially very soggy chocolate cake with chocolate icing and not a lot else in it, is essential to health and prevents all kinds of bad diseases. But this is not generally known nowadays. Back to the story.

Chocolatina looked soulfully at the chocolate cake. Then she looked mournfully at the polystyrene. "I did eat most of it," she said.

There were several minutes of silence during which Angelika frowned. "No wonder you're thin if you don't finish your main course," she said. More silence. Chocolatina knew that she wouldn't get her own way by making a scene, so she looked as sweet and pleading as she could. "Please please please," she pleaded. Finally Angelika gave in. "Just this once," she said.

Chocolatina knew she'd be expected to eat the whole cake and not just the chocolate part, but she had a special way of sucking the chocolate off and crumbling the biscuity bit just enough that most of it disintegrated into crumbs, which could be scattered thinly around the plate. Her mouth watered as she prepared for the first sucky bite.

IT WAS HORRIBLE! And the biscuity bit wouldn't disintegrate. It felt like a concrete block in her fist.

"Don't you like your carob bar?" Angelika asked. "You made such a fuss about wanting to eat it!"

"Carob?" Chocolatina whispered in distraught anguish.

"Yes. Chocolate is so bad for you because it contains stimulants, and affects the colour of your aura. I never eat it. Carob is a healthy alternative to chocolate," Angelika explained patiently.

"CAROB BAR? CAROB BAR?" I told you Chocolatina was a girl who didn't stand any nonsense. She leapt onto the table, brandishing the carob bar, her natural leather sandals dirtying the plastic table cloth and crushing the remains of her Japanese polystyrene. "What is wrong," she addressed the astonished crowd of slightly frayed middle class hippies, "with a substance lovingly harvested in sustainable rainforests by indigenous tribes with interesting cultures?" Chocolatina, as well as being a wizz at mental arithmetic, knew a lot of long words.

"Chocolate, that food of heaven, drunk by the Aztecs on their way to Teotihuacan to look for their ancestral gods? A substance you can sink your teeth into, confident of being transported halfway to paradise in one bite, a reminder of things divine, an intimation of higher states of consciousness, a foretaste of heavenly bliss?" Her voice rose in a tide of passion, echoing around the cafe with its gaping hippies. In a long embarrassed moment of dead silence someone dropped a spoon, and a wild looking toddler said "j'accuse" (or it might have been "gaga" - I'm not sure).

She carried on: "What other substance has such properties and is yet so free of harmful and vicious qualities, that does not lead to crime, disease or degradation, that can be enjoyed quietly alone or shared with friends, a substance almost universally acceptable as a gift or a token of love? Something, most of all, that brings a smile to the cheeks of children?"

Chocolatina paused for dramatic effect, every nuance of her speech measured for its effect on the aghast people, with their ethnic hats and faded jeans. Somewhere a set of beads with little Indian bells on jingled timidly, and a spirit catcher made out of an old clothes hanger and some wool quivered in the window. Someone coughed nervously. Chocolatina resumed with her voice quieter, every word now seeming addressed directly to each person in the café.

"Who would be so puritanical," she reasoned, "so spiritually inspissated, so dried up in their hearts, as to deny, in this world of pain, a brief respite from worldly cares afforded by cocoa products?" She looked around at adult faces now ridden with guilt and uncertainty. "Not only for adults," she went on, preparing the coup de grâce, "but also, and indeed especially, because childhood is not sweet, but hard, for *children*. Who is it, I say, that is so degraded that they hate the innocence of children with such a meanness, such a warped sensibility, with, I say, such an evil passion, as to deny them - chocolate?"

Not waiting for the crowd to recover, she leapt from the table, laying about her with the carob bar which crashed through the food counter as though it were a concrete block dropping through balsa wood. The incense burner fell backwards onto the pile of Japanese polystyrene, which exploded in a 'whoomf' of intense yellow sooty fire. One by one the flaming polystyrene things floated to the ceiling, setting fire to the paper lampshades on the way. As the hippies scattered in terror, dragging their wild looking toddlers after them, all the remaining carob bars collapsed together in a heap, the intense gravitational force caused by their very heavy structure causing a black hole in the middle of the wreckage. Chocolatina grabbed Angelika's hand

and pulled with main force as Angelika's Guatemalan shawl was sucked from her shoulders with a sickening slurping sound into the whirlpool of the black hole, and as they reached the street the entire café with all its contents disappeared into another dimension, leaving a very neat vacant lot between the Viennese coffee house and the chocolate shop.

Which just goes to show you shouldn't lose your temper, even if you are in the right (I think).

Love in Space – a drabble

A drabble is a 100-word novel. I have counted hyphenated words as two words.

The curves of her body under her skin-tight spacesuit reflected the alien sun in streaks of laser-like intensity.

I set my phaser to *stun*.

Her speech translated through the UniTalk: "You are a fine specimen. You can be my mate on a permanent basis, then you are free to go. I shall not eat you this time."

She came closer. Before I could think she had grabbed my phaser. It went off. I spent the next year in her dome. I didn't understand anything that happened to me during that time. My phaser went off almost every hour.

The true story of Wolf and Redcap and how vengeance was wreaked on the Woodcutter

The scar in his belly still ached, but he could live with that. The Woodcutter had taken Redcap, and that left Wolf with restless nights and an anger that gnawed.

She-Wolf was a little bit in love with Wolf. She had warned Wolf not to get involved with Redcap, to be satisfied with being Wolf by day and howling in the forest jazz combo at night. Anything else would lead to trouble. Keep out of the way of the Woodcutter, too. He does a sideline in wolfskin coats. But for Wolf there was something missing, and what he had wasn't enough.

When he had first seen Redcap, picking flowers near the woods with two of her friends, she had immediately struck him as different. Three girls chatting and smiling, yet only one of them with a face that was not all surface. The other two existed as their shining eyes, their animation over whatever trivia of the moment had seized them, their dimpled smiles. She had a face which was not the emotions it expressed, but through which they passed, as though that body concealed a world. Those unadorned lips, no tension spoiling their perfect form. Those eyes, impassive, innocent, impossibly beautiful. To the other two, she was one of them, but to Wolf, she was something mysterious, a being of another ilk.

One day her two friends had errands elsewhere, and they left. Redcap picked up her basket and ventured into the woods. Wolf moved from one tree to the next, following her for a while without being seen. Eventually, as if by accident, he had walked onto the same path and greeted her. They walked for a while side by side, and talked.

Wolf, thinking back on it later, understood that his motives had not been entirely pure. By night he dreamed of her face, of her hidden being, of a world he would like to enter, be part of, she, a garden in Arcadia. He would cherish her, protect her from the treacherous world in which he knew too well how to survive. She would complete him, or perhaps he would disappear altogether into her greater being. By day he remembered her well-formed legs, imagined her young breasts, formed the outline of her body from the memory of how her skirt and blouse had caressed it. He wanted to eat her up.

What sensible mother sends her daughter out on her own into the woods? It was to protect her that

Wolf had walked by her side, talked of who knows what, every word a meaningless delight, every word now forgotten, only the memory of her presence burned into his soul. Passing the Woodcutter's hut, Wolf had seen him staring through the window, understood that peeping villain from the darkness in his own heart.

Then they had glimpsed Baba Yaga's hut in the distance. What did you expect, that an honest grandmother lives in the middle of a forest? The whole set-up was suspicious from the beginning. The very fence posts had skulls on top of them and the hut was crooked. It did not exactly stand on chicken legs, but neither did it stand properly on the ground, being supported by random pieces of wood, some looking like bones. Baba Yaga had a reputation for eating everyone.

Are you sure this is the right place? Wolf had asked her. Oh yes, she had replied, her smile innocent of any sense of danger.

I was absorbed in love and fascinated by desire, he thought. That is why I didn't notice that the Woodcutter had crept round by another route, I hadn't seen him creep behind the trees, I hadn't heard the latch of Baba Yaga's back door.

Well, here we must part, Wolf had said. Redcap smiled at him, looked at him with the sweet expression that was habitual to her, but which Wolf believed to signal love. Then Wolf had also crept unseen through Baba Yaga's back door.

Tap tap! He could hear Redcap knocking at the front door.

Terror gripped him. Baba Yaga may have been small but she was not to be trifled with. He peered round the door-frame of the scullery and there in the half-darkness he could make out Baba Yaga's back as she slouched towards the front door. Only later was he to find out that the Woodcutter had hidden in the cupboard like the cowardly villain he was. Hiding in cupboards is not the way of wolves.

There had been only this moment in which to act. He leaped. Baba Yaga turned, saw him in mid-flight and shrieked a curse. Suddenly there was no Baba Yaga. A rat scurried across the floor towards a hole in the wall. Wolf twisted his body, jaws wide, and swallowed the rat whole as his front paws hit the ground.

Tap tap!

Already his insides began to ache horribly.

Tap tap!

Quickly he opened the cupboard and rummaged among the dirty clothes that hung and rested in screwed up piles, failing to see the Woodcutter clutching his axe and trembling in his wolfskin coat.

Wolf put on a selection of what he could find, mainly a large nightcap that would at least cover his ears. It was dark indoors, and Baba Yaga was no oil painting. Redcap would not notice.

Tap tap!

Wolf rushed into the bed, covering his hairy legs with the duvet covered in spiders. "Come in! The door is open!"

There was Redcap, framed with light, standing with her basket covered in a gingham cloth. Wolf's heart melted, his loins filled with desire and his belly twisted in pain. She stepped into the darkness, came over to the bed, and sat down by the bedside. The light from the open door reflected softly from the bedsheets onto that face, the face of a radiant being, a face that could convert atheists.

The belly pain gripped him in a vicious colic, but it meant nothing. He was in an agony of love, a pain that overwhelmed everything. He wanted to grab her, take her to him, possess her, eat her up. She was so close.

She stared at his face, making out in the shadows only the glint in his eyes.

"What big eyes you have, grandmother!"

"I only want to see you." His nightcap came loose as he shifted in pain.

"What big ears you have!"

"I only want to hear you." He smiled.

"Your teeth are bigger than I remember."

Redcap did make a lot of personal remarks. But he could not bring himself to rebuke her. He wanted her. He could have grabbed her in a moment. Yet he knew also that if he grabbed her he would lose her forever. Love prevented him.

Then the Woodcutter chose to burst out of the cupboard wielding his axe. Redcap started back in horror as the axe, aimed at Wolf's heart, cleft instead his belly as Wolf attempted to jump out of the way. A bloodied rat jumped out and scuttled across the floor leaving a red trail as Wolf turned and leaped towards the Woodcutter. The Woodcutter grabbed the now blood-spattered Redcap by the wrist and dragged her towards the door. Wolf attempted to run after them, then he blacked out.

When he came round he was back in bed and Baba Yaga was standing over him. A continuous pain ran through him. He gingerly felt his belly and found to his surprise that it was bandaged.

"I don't eat creatures who are blessed, and you are half-blessed. You are of a different ilk, and might upset my digestion," Baba Yaga was saying. "Still, I reserve the right."

Wolf had stayed with Baba Yaga for several weeks, healing and plotting. She bustled about like a harmless farmer's wife, feeding and nurturing him. The food was good and he started to put on weight. Wolf worried about this occasionally, but then, he was getting better. Surely he could just run out of the door whenever he felt like it? Considering Baba Yaga's reputation though, Wolf decided that the best plan was to leave unexpectedly, to creep out at night when Baba Yaga was out flying about in her pestle and mortar. Baba Yaga was too nice and it put him in mind of the story about the gingerbread house.

One night at full moon Wolf decided to leave. He waited until he heard Baba Yaga's cackle as she flew off. He crept out of bed. The ache in his belly was bearable now. Deal with the Woodcutter. That was next. Then rescue Redcap. Padding softly out of the door, he sniffed the cold forest air. Then across the dry leaves, making no more sound than the rustling wind. From somewhere in the darkness came an eerie howl, like someone in pain.

"Don't think I can't see you!" Baba Yaga's voice came from nowhere. He shook himself and his hair stood on end. But she did not appear and she did not stop him as he ventured further into the wood. On he went, picking and sniffing his way back towards the Woodcutter's hut.

There in the clearing was She-Wolf howling, her leg held in a cruel trap. Out of his hut came the Woodcutter, swinging his axe. Swifter than thought Wolf sprang, his snarling jaws slicing through the air towards Woodcutter's throat, oblivious of that axe. At the same moment cutting the forest air a sharp cackle from up in the trees.

"Go lovely in a pie!"

Woodcutter looked up, fell back, eyes wide, arms flailing, axe handle slipping up out of his hand, body falling, axe arcing up and descending, slitting his throat before even hair or tooth or spittle of Wolf touched him. Wolf stopped, astonished. Then gentle as leaf-fall Baba Yaga rowed the mortar down from the treetops. "Vengeance is mine!"

Wolf cried out, "The saying is, 'Vengeance is mine, *saith the Lord.*'"

"The point is, it's not yours. Hahahahaha!"

Turning, Wolf used his jaws to open the trap, and She-Wolf limped out, circled him once then sat, nuzzling against him.

At that moment Redcap emerged from the hut, bedraggled and still blood-spattered but beautiful as ever. "It's not so much me you love as the beauty in your own heart," she said. "As for your lust, God will provide."

He felt She-Wolf's soft fur and heard her throaty growl. He put a paw gently on her shoulder. Later he took up jazz and they played wild sax all night, every night.

The future son-in-law

For a long time my eldest daughter had no boyfriend. I once asked her if she was gay. "No, daddy," she replied. It turns out she is just picky. Quite right. One doesn't want one's daughter marrying any old riff-raff.

Now she has a long-time partner of whom I thoroughly approve. However I think he is a little in awe of me.

I trust when he decides to propose to her he will come and inform me of the fact. I shall sit in a large armchair but keep him standing. I shall have a pipe ready for the occasion, even though I don't smoke. I shall offer him sherry, just to make it more awkward.

"Now then, what was it you wanted to tell me?"

Detail from Hieronymus Bosch (c.1450-1516),
The Garden of Earthly Delights

Hieronymus Bosch: The Garden of Earthly Delights

Huge berries for food,
Pomegranates for houses,
They dance in the nude
With lustless carouses.
Crowds like our thoughts
Drift on for miles
And no-one's distraught,
But nobody smiles.

A big porcupine
In a black-dappled bubble
With his prickly behind
Tries to stay out of trouble
And with joy or with pain
Nobody is stricken
And a naked man
Rides a four-legged chicken.

Senseless ends,
Unconscious wishes:
Metal mermen
Feed the fishes.

Rivers form pathways
Round tortured confections
With spires architectural
And open pink doorways
And rocky erections
(Whose meaning's conjectural).

When our minds start to drift,
And we're seeing strange sights,
Then we're back in the Garden
Of Earthly Delights.
And all this that seems –
To real sense is refractory,
And pleasure in dreams
Strangely unsatisfactory.

What is the cost
Of these constant near-misses?
Real desire is lost
And nobody kisses.

Some people said
He was on some stuff
But Bosch shook his head,
Said, 'Life's mad enough.'

Diving into the Library*

The shower's broken. Into the library
You dive, your young form washed by dusty tomes,
Their old dry pages swell a paper sea,
Your smooth skin bathes in literary foams.

The book of you perhaps I shall not find
Yet printed, but I cannot help confess
With what artistic pleasure I should bind
Your own slim volume in my private press.

Acknowledgments: all things your smile can reach;
Contents: a list of promised prosody
Pointing to moist verses, cleansing each
Round limb and mound and valley of your body.

Your hidden part's not indexed in this book –
O would that I could take you home, and look.

---

* I don't remember what prompted this. It was a long time ago.

Ludwig Hammer, private eye

Editor's note: It is said that the philosopher Ludwig Wittgenstein decided that since he had solved all the problems of philosophy, he would devote his spare time to reading detective novels. Later an obscure Argentine writer, Ramón Luis Fabricante de la Vela, took up the challenge of writing philosophical detective novels, of which only one was ever published and is now hard to find. A battered copy was discovered by Milton Marmalade while browsing in the second-hand book section of an Oxfam charity shop.

From Ludwig Hammer, Private Eye, by Ramón Luis Fabricante de la Vela, Chapter 23, translated from the Spanish by Lola Tabasco and Milton Marmalade.

After the bust-up I needed somewhere to cool off. I found myself in a narrow alley in the Greek quarter. It was raining. There were lights on in a small bar with a neon sign – Petros' place. I went in and ordered a double bourbon.

The guy behind the bar looked old, but in that kinda way where you can't really tell how old he is –

in that light he could've been fifty or a hundred and fifty. He moved slowly. I snapped at him to make it quick – maybe my nerves were getting to me.

"Endaxi." He pushed the drink in front of me, calm as a cat sleeping off the cream. "Chairos einai. There is plenty time."

"What do you know about it?" I barked. For all I knew there were more of the Metaphysics gang right around the corner.

"Is always time here, boss." He had a gentle look in his eyes I don't often see in this town. "In Petros' bar a drink can last all afternoon. Time – it all depend on your point of view."

I downed a gulp of the bourbon – the fire in my throat seemed to clear my head. There were two customers at the table by the window, a couple of lovers trying to save money on a night out maybe, otherwise the place was empty. The old guy mopped the counter as though mopping mattered more than the result.

Time is something you can talk about. It's not metaphysics, it's real, like the ticking of the clock over the bar. You can measure it. And time was running out – either for the Metaphysics gang or for me.

"You look my clock. It do you no good." I started – the old guy seemed to read my mind. "You don't measure time by my clock. Is why: if time go fast, my clock go fast. If time go slow, like now, my clock go slow too."

His eyes looked through me rather than at me. I looked at my glass – it was empty. I glanced at the clock – the hands hadn't moved. "Another double," I rasped.

"My name is Parmenides, but people call me Petros." I hadn't asked, but all the same I told him my name was Leo. I didn't want anyone on my tail, and I might have to come back there. "Pleased to meet you, Petros."

"My friend 'Eraclitos, he say you can never come back here." He guessed my thoughts again. Coincidence, but it gave me the creeps. Petros's face broke into a thousand laugh lines. "But I say, Petros' place always here. You, Mr Leo, will always be here."

"You're wrong there. I'm leaving soon."

"Mr Leo, let me show you something." He rummaged under the counter, and came out with a huge dusty roll of cloth. He unwound part of it on the bar. It was an old tapestry with thousands of tiny pictures woven all over it. Something in Greek was written along the edges. For a moment he stared at it. Suddenly his finger jabbed into the middle of the cloth. "Look," he said.

I squinted closely where the old man's finger creased the stained fabric. There was a tiny image of a guy in a raincoat with the collar turned up leaning against a bar, and an old guy mopping it – you get the deal. A little further along I could see the guy in the raincoat again, facing down some hoods with a vanload of philosophy books, but what happened next was hidden under the roll of cloth. Somewhere to one side a little cloth couple were in her apartment with the lights off.

Petros rolled up the cloth and hid it back under the counter. "You see, I right and 'Eraclitos wrong. You always here. Petros' bar always exist."

I'd had enough. I walked out into the rain. I never went back to Petros' bar, and when I went down the alley six months later, there was a Starbucks there, and Petros' bar had gone.

Infinity Station

*Dedicated to my old maths teacher, J. M. ('Jim')
Turner, Henley Grammar School, some time a long
time ago.*

All mathematicians want to go to infinity, to see
the place where all the parallel lines meet. There is a
station there called, logically enough, Infinity
Station, but no trains. You have to go on foot the
last few miles, because of a problem with the railway
tracks.*

---

* Mr Turner was reported in the school magazine as having said,
"Infinity is a very long way. Unfortunately we can't go there."
What he actually said was that it's not a place where you can go,
and there are no mathematicians there waving their arms
excitedly and saying, "Look at all the parallel lines crossing!"

Silly limericks about mathematicians

A young girl called Sophie Germain*
Had a fever with math on the brain
One night in delirium
She proved Fermat's last theorem
Then woke up and forgot it again.

---

* Sophie Germain (1776 – 1831). Her parents denied her a warm
nightie and a fire as they felt her preoccupation with
mathematics was unsuitable for a girl, imagining she would
therefore stay tucked up in bed. She used to work by candlelight
wrapped in bedclothes. According to Lynn M. Osen's *Women in
Mathematics,* when her parents found Sophie 'asleep at her desk
in the morning, the ink frozen in the ink horn and her slate
covered with calculations,' they finally realised that girls can
think. She did important early work on proving Fermat's Last
Theorem, but the full proof was not established until 1994.

An ancient Greek sage called Pythagoras*
Made theorems of math that would stagger us
He ate never a bean
For he found them obscene
But thought nothing of eating asparagus.

---

* Pythagoras was reputedly a vegetarian and members of his cult
were forbidden to eat beans. Some say this was because beans
resemble testicles, but there is no compelling evidence for this
explanation, which in any case begs the question. I mean, beans
also resemble kidneys but that doesn't stop people eating
steak-and-kidney pie (or beans). My own theory is that he used
beans for developing number theory and by the time he had
finished with them they were too grubby to cook with. This
limerick has no real merit other than in finding rhymes for
Pythagoras.

The mathematician Cantor*
Met a lady he liked more and more
"I'd go to infinity
To take your virginity
To infinity and a bit more."

---

* Georg Cantor (1845-1918) found out that there are infinite
things that are bigger than other infinite things, even though
both are infinite (look up Cantor's diagonal proof, which is
surprisingly easy to understand if properly explained). Anyway, he
did marry but the limerick is otherwise fictional. It is said that
during his honeymoon he spent a lot of time discussing
mathematics with a chum. If I had a hot wife waiting for me all
naked in bed I don't think I'd be saying, "Just off for a bit of set
theory, dear!" Maybe that's why I'm not a mathematician.

The Secret of the Universe Research

You have a sealed envelope. You are to deliver it to
the man who lives at the top of the Shard, London.
His name is Hieronymus Phniggs and his office is
called Secret of the Universe Research.

Hieronymus Phniggs understands that living at
the highest point in London, which is a sacred city,
will help him in his research. The pointiness of the
Shard is an additional attraction, as it is created at
the exact angle that, according to various arcane
calculations, will concentrate cosmic energy most
effectively.

You ascend in the high speed lift, the envelope in
your inner jacket pocket. At the 68th floor you
emerge with the sightseers to the viewing area.
From here you take a further lift and finally stairs to
floor 84. There is a door with an intercom. You
press the button and the door opens with a buzzing
sound without anyone answering.

As a consequence of living at the top of the Shard,
the apartment, which is also Phniggs's office, has
unusual geometry. The lowest floor in which you
now find yourself is a more-or-less normal space,
albeit with the walls tilted in and entirely of glass.
You have the unnerving impression that you might

walk out into the sky in a moment of inattention, perhaps in the act of looking for a lost fountain pen behind a sofa.

You reflect that this would not be the worst way to die, arguably, in that the view would be phenomenal. Also the long descent would allow sufficient time to bring your being into harmony with whatever the Secret of the Universe is, whether by prayer or stoical acceptance. You might also consider Wittgenstein's dictum that death is not an event in life, just as the visual field, although limited, does not have an edge. You would have time on the way down to open the envelope which might perhaps contain the actual Secret. These considerations do not however altogether alleviate a feeling of vertigo.

You ascend a spiral staircase set into the centre of the room. The second to top floor, as anyone with a grasp of three-dimensional geometry will have realised already, is slightly smaller and in the form of a truncated cone. It is lined with bookcases, all tilting in so that you are enveloped in tiers of books. You feel that the books might fall on you at any moment, and you want to adopt the posture of Alice fending off a shower of cards at the end of *Wonderland*. The number of books is very large.

In the centre the spiral staircase continues upwards to a hole in the ceiling. No doubt this serves the dual purpose of allowing access to the top floor and also to the books on the top shelves. On the way up you pick one out at random. It opens at an illustration: a large calligraphy of the Arabic letter *kun*. Be. You put it back. You reach behind you without looking and pull out another book, The Making of Honey. You open it and it falls to a picture of a bee. You try another and it is the Koran: 'He need only say Be, and it is.' And again, Bismillah. In the name of the One who Is. Beginning with the English letter B. One more: The Tibetan Book of the Dead. 'Let all beings awaken *right now*.'

The spiral staircase ends. Next to it is an ancient wooden desk with an attached bench, done in a medieval style and resembling that of Saint Jerome in his study.

Hieronymus Phniggs is an old man with a full head of white hair and a white beard. The hair and beard look dry and slightly dishevelled. His face is thin and his eyes, although alert, have a kind of absence to them, as though he is not quite there. He smiles at you in a way that doesn't put you at your ease, although you feel it should. It is a smile that has forgotten the meaning of smiling.

"Well, sit down." He gestures to a small stool on which you sit, rather uncomfortably. Yet the discomfort has more to do with Phniggs than it does with the stool.

"I think this is what you have been looking for." You hand him the envelope. He puts it on the desk, unopened.

"Thank you. Most kind."

You were expecting him to be a little more excited than that.

"I think it's what you have been looking for all your life," you say, trying to bring forth more of a response.

"Mm, well, who can tell?" A look of slight anxiety crosses his face, and he puts the envelope to one side.

He offers tea, and you accept, out of politeness I suppose, and also from the hope that he will open the envelope. Eventually the tea is finished, and you stand up to leave. You extend a hand and he takes yours and gives it a brief shake. You turn and start back down the spiral staircase, out onto the landing and back down to the ordinary world of London Bridge Station.

The world is strangely bright.

We are still birds, and children of the sky

Swims a gloomy fish through muddy weeds,
There hides the flickering tail-fin of despair;
The bottom-dweller on detritus feeds:
A Something sees all this, and is not there.

Between the half-lit gloomy depths and air
Exists a surface shimmering and free:
Beneath this subtle boundary despair
Drifts through an imaginary sea.

We looked below and fancied ourselves fishes;
Our vision caught, we understood not why
Our airy state had turned to brine-worn wishes;
We are still birds, and children of the sky.

Using Epimenides' paradox against hostile alien robots

Captain Steve Thrust saw it first.

"Look out! A hostile alien robot armed with a disintegrator ray!"

Brains wobbled a little but remained calm. An alien sun gleamed on the polished hull of the spaceship. In the distance the silhouette of a mechanical alien could be seen advancing towards them steadily.

"I – I think there's something about this in the Starfleet Manual," Brains ventured. He pulled the little electronic book from a pocket in his utility belt and flipped it open. It responded to his eye movements, indexes and submenus flashing across the screen until the image stabilised.

"Ah! Here it is: 'Hostile alien robots: use Epimenides' paradox. Say, 'All Earthlings are consistent liars.'"

"How does that help us?" Steve Thrust was the kind of man for whom a blast with a ray gun from mid-air while executing a kung-fu move was better than thinking.

Brains continued: "Uh, quoting the manual, 'Then the robot will say, 'If you are a consistent liar, then you must be lying now, therefore it is a lie that you are a consistent liar, so you must be telling the truth at least sometimes. If you are telling the truth now then it must be true that you are a consistent liar, therefore you must be lying now...' and so on. This will cause them to say 'does not compute' at higher and higher pitch while their eyes roll about and steam comes out of their ears. During this time they will not be able to use their disintegrator rays. Then their heads will blow off.'"

"Good thinking Brains!" Thrust's jaw set in a steely heroic grin as the robot advanced within a few yards.

"Let nothing stand in my path! Resistance is feudal!" it said in a tinny voice with a distinct American accent.

Thrust leaned nonchalantly on the side of the spaceship and drawled, "All Earthlings are consistent liars."

The robot hesitated, then: "Hah! That - old - thing! It's just words. I work to uninterpreted strings, and this output only appears to have meaning for you, but to me, it has no meaning. So I shall now deliver you to Fang the Frightful!"

Brains frowned. "Uh – not logical, Captain," he said.

Alexander Beetle

Alexander, name of Beetle
Lived on Tate and Lyle's treacle
He said, "this mode of life is tricky
Because it makes my feelers sticky;
Besides the cost is really sinful
At fourpence ha'penny a tinful,
And so to earn an honest crust
A well-paid business is a must.
Yes! What about some beetle lasses
Who'd share with me my fine molasses?
For beetle dames there must be many
Who would admire my sweet antennae!
So I'll attract fine beetle dames-es
To my emporium in St James's."
His cunning shop display reflected
Delights within to be expected,
Thus with a green and golden tin
Alexander lured them in.

– not by A. A. Milne at all.

Freud and the Wolf Man

Note to readers: this is a silly story and is not intended to represent any actual historical events.

One day as Sigmund Freud was psychoanalysing the person he was later to write up as 'the Wolf Man,' he noticed something odd about his patient's ears.

Freud blinked and turned his gaze to the peaceful Viennese street beyond the window, as if to anchor himself better in reality. Somewhere a cat miaowed. Then he returned his gaze to the back of the Wolf Man's head. His patient was still lying on the couch facing away from the analyst, as Dr Freud always arranged it. The light from the window shone through the Wolf Man's ears, and yes, there definitely was a tuft of orange hair growing out of them. Not from the ear canals, as in the case of many men who neglect details of their personal appearance, but from the very tops of the auricles. The ears were a bit pointy, too.

Freud wondered that he had never noticed this before.

"Perhaps I never saw it because I wasn't expecting it to be the case," he mused silently to himself. Meanwhile the wolf man continued to talk to the ceiling. The doctor's pen still hovered over his notepad, but it hardly mattered if his notes ceased for a while since patients tend to be repetitive, especially the Wolf Man. Like wolves really. A limited range of preoccupations. Fantasies about eating people, mostly without cooking them first.

"But if I didn't notice it before, why would I suddenly notice it now?" Freud continued to think, his brow furrowed. He liked to analyse everything. After all, the whole science of psychoanalysis would start from the great doctor's own self-analysis, from which by apostolic succession all subsequent analysts take their authority.

"Perhaps it is because once my mother... ." But he couldn't think of anything his mother had done that could implicate her in his not noticing the Wolf Man's ears before but noticing them now. Come to think of it he didn't remember the Wolf Man's sideburns previously extending onto his cheeks with the luxuriance they now exhibited.

"...so you see I am no better at all..." the Wolf Man continued in a monotone rather like a growl, "and I have these urges to go into the forest and hunt innocent creatures and then swallow them whole..."

The doctor felt there was something even defiant about his patient. Perhaps he didn't want to get better at all. Perhaps all this was a waste of time. But on the other hand he was a good payer.

Suddenly Freud remembered with a start that his next patient would already be waiting as she was always early. She would be sitting primly in the waiting room holding the little basket she always carried and wearing her little red cap. What was in the basket under that little gingham check cloth, he wondered?

He coughed. "Your session time is up," he said quietly. "Perhaps you would like to exit by the window? You can hop over onto the neighbour's fence from the window-ledge."

"Why would I want to do that?" enquired the Wolf Man.

"Why would you want to do that? Ach! It is interesting that you always try to extend your session time by one last question! We can talk about it next time."

With that the Wolf Man jumped off the couch and onto the window-ledge on all fours, pausing briefly to give the doctor a backward glance with his fierce wolfish eyes, and then jumped out of sight.

The sound of a cat suddenly not miaowing could be heard.

Sir Henry Herring's account of St Doris Island[*]

Thus we landed in severall small boats leaving the Hinde at anchor some distance from the shore, on account of the gentle slope of the bottom. It was a verdant iland all set around with fronded trees and in the midst a great volcano, the which we thought extinct, there being no show of smoke or fire therefrom.

Drake at once leapt from the boat and planted the flagge of England in the sand, claiming the iland for Gloriana our gracious Majestie Queene Elizabeth. We then on our knees offered up a prayer to Almightie God for our safe deliverance to this place,

---

* From chapter 16 of *A Mermaid in the Bath* by Milton Marmalade, in which our hero reads from an old book, 'Seynt Doris, an Ilande in ye Westerne Indies, its Historie Geographie & divers Marvells founde therein together with a Description of its Aboriginall Salvages, set down in all Veritie by Henry Herring, Earl of a Bit of Cornwall and not the Other Bit, who went there with Francis Drake, Kt. in the XXI year of the reine of Her Glorious Majestie Queen Elizabeth whom God preserve. Printed and sold at St. Doris-by-the-Fishmonger Churchyard, London MDLXXXXIX.

and I also quietly did offer thanks to our own Seynte Doris, thinking that if I were to pray out loud some might think me a Catholick, but knowing in my hart that I am a true Protestant and loyal subject of the Queene of England.

What shall we call this place? inquired Drake. I made bold to say it should be called Seynte Doris as many of the crew were from my Bit of Cornwall and therefore such a name were fitting.

Ha, quoth Drake, thou shalt have thy way Fisheface (for thus he did call me in jeste on account of my name of Herring, that being a fishe), and so did I humbly accept the jeste with a smile so that the iland could be thus named. For by occasion humilitie can achieve more than the posturing of coxcombs.

Searching about we did find many things that were good to eat, such as the fleshe of huge woody nuts that must needs be cleaved with a sword, sea weed that when cooked put us in mind of the cabbage that was the customary fare of our school dayes, and a great quantity of fishes. Thus hungry and weary from our travells we did make a feast on the beach.

Now I must tell of the most great marvell of that place, hearing the which the honest reader may well doubt of my veracitie. Honest Cornishmen have spoken of suchlike things and been laughed to scorne, thus to this day they do hold their tongues. E'en so I shall now set forth the truth of the matter, let he who will, gainsay it. If thou believe it, so, and if not, then do as thou wilt.

The cooking of the fishes did cause such a wondrous pleasant smell that presently came some of the natives of that land most curious to see what should be occurring on their beach. But came they not from the land but from the sea, and wonder to behold they were of the form of beautiful maidens, clothed scantilie in sea weed and otherwise in little more than the apparell in which they had been borne.

This caused a most mightie stirring among the sailors, but Drake did not wish to mar the reign of her Majestie upon this new Dominion with any kind of impolitick controversie, so he did order the crew to throw buckets of water over each other untill their vegetable passions be safely diminished to proportions proper for social intercourse. This did indeed dampen the sailors ardour, though we nobles were much discomfited by the persistence of water in our codpieces.

Thus calmed into gentilnesse the sailors intreated the maidens with all civilitie to join them in the feast, whereupon some of the maidens lifted themselves onto rocks nearby but came no further in, the reason being much apparent by that their thighs and legges were joined into the form of fishey tails.

At this some did say that this was the worke of the Evil One but others said that nothing so beautiful could be made by the Lord of Darknesse for it is not in his power to do thus and therefore it is godly. At this all the mermaids, for such they were, began to sing a most melodious and plaintive song so that even the rudest member of the crew was much affected by it.

During all our sojourn on that iland peaceful relations persisted between the sailors and the mermaids, the sailors being much changed in their manners and showing much courtesie. By moonlight each would wade to the rock of his favourite maid and feed her with fishe the which he had first cooked with spices on the fire. She in turn would sing for him at which he would gaze upon her most tenderlie.

At length the sailors began to teach the mermaids to speak in their own tongue, some in English and some in the Cornish or Kernewek as it is called. Some of the sailors claimed afterward that their mermaids spoke the Kernewek passing well, which did surprise them greatly. For their part the mermaids did teach the sailors some words of their own language, which however had no ready translations into English or Cornish and which the sailors could but understand when the mermaids spoke it. For my part I could only remember the speech of mermaids at dawn for at other times it left no trace on my memory.

Nor was I unaffected by all this but found myself with a deep affection for one of the mermaids. I never knew her name but she sang to me and then I understood many things that I have since forgot. Whether it be folly or no I must one day return to that iland, for there it is certaine my hart remains. For her part I know that she will not forget me, though I know not how I deserve it.

After many dayes passed in replenishing the stores of the ship and mending our bodies and most of all our soules, for such was the effect of the mermaids on all of us, Drake did address the crew thus:

It is not for idlenesse that Her Majestie hath entrusted me with this journey, but for to enrich oure nation with all manner of foreign things, not least by the plundering of Spanish gold. Therefore must we leave this iland on the morrow.

This speche did the sailors receive with much lamentation, albeit talk of gold did begin to revive their avarice. Therefore did Drake order an extra ration of rum and full many of the crew forgot their mermaids that night and did slepe until dawn.

For myself no gold and no rum could quench the longing in my brest and I did steal away to my mermaid, who seemed to understand that we must parte, and sang so sweetlie that I thought I should dye, nor would such a fate at such a time have been unwelcome.

Heraclitus's Railway Adventure

A short play or interlude in which we play with some ideas of pre-Socratic philosophy in relation to the problem of time and change and the meaning of the word 'now.' What is the relation between 'now' and consciousness? Is there a physical meaning to the word 'now'?

Characters:

Heraclitus, a philosopher who says you can never step into the same river twice;

Parmenides, a philosopher who says that everything is always the same and that change is impossible;

Ariadne, an immortal.

Act 1, Scene 1

Paddington Station, London

Heraclitus: Parmenides! It's true, you do look awesome, just as Socrates said after he met you - or after he will meet you at some time in the future.

Parmenides: Well, Heraclitus you old rascal, it's my job to say that nothing changes. So in a sense that meeting with Socrates already exists, even though I don't know about it yet. But that doesn't give you an excuse to indulge in wild anachronisms. Anyway, what are you doing here at Paddington Station?

H: See, I have a one way ticket to Swansea!

P: Why a one way ticket to Swansea?

H: Well, it's some new rule. The railway company is so bad at giving out correct ticket pricing information, what with all the Awaydays, Family Railcards, Apex Advance Booking Stopover Returns, Bring a Dog and Your Bicycle Travels Free, and Student Pensioner Special Fares (only available on trains passing through Watford on the fifth Tuesday in February), that they've decided to simplify the system. One way tickets only. And you're not allowed to return to the station where you purchased your ticket. The railway company finds this cuts down on the number of complaints.

P: No, I mean, why Swansea?

H: Because swans are the most beautiful of birds. They are owned by the British Crown and so they don't get eaten, thus they are symbolic of the only part of the soul that is immortal, the psyche. Also, don't forget that Zeus came to Leda in the form of a swan. (Did you know by the way that swans, unlike other birds, actually do have penises? I read that on the internet.) And before you ask, the sea, THALASSA, is in the blood of all Greeks. Thus, Swansea represents the immortal soul swimming in the sea of time, immutable beauty in the midst of that which incessantly changes.

P: You do realise that Swansea is in South Wales?

H: Oh.

P: I'm going to Birmingham myself. The second city of the Hyperboreans! The Athens of the Midlands, they tell me!

H: Well, since everything changes, I expect I'll end up somewhere entirely different from Swansea anyway. I'd like to come along with you, share your adventure, and perhaps persuade you that everything is in constant movement, which should be easy on the railway.

P: Be my guest. But you're wrong about the railway. Look, right here where we're standing is a map of the line. You can see that once you're on the train you'll end up in Swansea eventually.

H: Yes, everything moves and changes. Soon these iron pillars and the glass roof will be no more, and the landscape will blur and transform itself.

P: Indeed, but it will only appear to do so as you rush past. And at the end of the line you will arrive at Swansea, which has always been there, and always will be there. Swansea exists now, although you cannot see it, like a myth, ever the same.

H: Just as in mythological time Zeus and Leda are always... You have a point there.

P: We'll have to separate at Reading General where I change for Birmingham. Once the ticket is printed, nothing can be done to alter it.

H: The moving finger writes, and having writ, moves on... as someone will once say.

P: I see you're coming round to my point of view a little, at least as far as the past is concerned?

H: The moving finger is always writing a new line...

P: It was always going to be the case that the 12.03 would leave at 12.03, so we'd better get on board!

H: You obviously haven't used the railway much recently. Well, this seems comfortable enough! I wonder if we'll travel fast enough to observe any Einsteinian relativistic phenomena?

Act 1, Scene 2

(The railway carriage, some time later...)

P: So you see, the appearance of Twyford station now rushing past us is merely a subjective effect of the fact that our consciousness is somehow connected to this railway carriage. In reality Twyford always exists, it is just that our consciousness is connected to 'now.'

H: Hmm... now Twyford exists, but according to my memory we passed Slough a while back, and Slough existed then. Of course I can still remember passing through Slough, but somehow the memory is less immediate, less real. If it were just as real, perhaps I wouldn't know whether we were now at Slough or Twyford?

P: Well, you would say you are conscious now, of Twyford passing by, but would you not say you were also conscious then, when Slough passed by? And if we were to mark on the railway line in felt pen all the moments you were conscious, wouldn't we be able to show an almost continuous felt pen line from Paddington to Twyford? Possibly even all the way to Swansea?

H: So if we call any moment I am conscious, 'now', are you saying that 'now' includes the whole felt pen line from Paddington to Swansea? That does rather seem to drain the meaning out of the word 'now,' doesn't it?

P: Yes, it's all caused by an illusion. I explained the whole thing in my second book, *The Way of Illusion*, only fragments of which are now extant. I discovered a truly remarkable proof, only unfortunately this railway compartment is too small to contain it.

H: At any rate, it does seem that our fate is in some way constrained. For example, I could not get out at Twyford to have a look around even if I wanted to.

Act 1, Scene 3

(*Later, on Reading station...*)

P: So you're saying you don't think Birmingham will be much cop?

H: Well they have Jasper Carrot I suppose...

P: I've been thinking. It's true that we couldn't have got off at Twyford, and I can't go to Swansea on this ticket, but what if we got on the slow train and got off at Streatley? They wouldn't have a ticket inspector except for the commuters, I shouldn't wonder.

H: Yes. Reading is one of those places that belongs to KAIROS time as well as CHRONOS – linear time. Kairos, the fork in the road. We can change trains here, go together to Streatley, and do a pub crawl.

P: And then we can go to the cheese shop, look around, think of the name of a cheese that they won't have, and then ask for it!

H: You mean, like Norwegian blue? Ahahaha!

P: Well, at any rate your sense of humour hasn't changed. Are we always the same, like Twyford and Swansea? Or does our ability to make use of KAIROS places (like Reading Station) mean that we too can change?

H: I expect Plato will have something to say about that (but he's just a kid now).

Act 2

A hill in Streatley

Heraclitus: To illustrate my point, I shall write a little note on this piece of cheese wrapper, and push this twig through it so... and so. There: it's just like those little labels gardeners used to make to show where they had planted the beans...

Parmenides: Apropos of which, they say Pythagoras never ate beans. Some people think it is because the soul can migrate into a bean at some stage, others because beans look like testicles, and others still because beans give one wind. Personally, I think he used beans to demonstrate the geometrical properties of numbers, and by the time he was finished they were too grubby to cook with.

H: Well, at any rate numbers do not change, I think we're agreed on that, and you can't cook with numbers. But everything down here changes all the time. That's what I'm saying. Anyway, I plant the little note in the ground, like this...

P: What's it say? Oh, you've written 'here and now.'

H: Exactly.

P: So?

H: Well, since we are, like peripatetic philosophers, walking around (in the present case up this hill so that we can picnic where we can see view of the river), in the next moment we see my little note a few paces off, and you can no longer read the writing. Here, I'll do another one.

P: What have you written this time?

H: The same. Only this time it is true, because it really is here and now, whereas the one I did before was there and then...

P: Although if you could read it from here it would probably still say 'here and now'...

H: ...and another one just here... and here...

(P. looks around in wordless awe at the scene coming into view below them)

H: ...and here...

P: Here's a good spot. Lucky I brought my green cloak: we'll sit on that.

H: See?

P: What?

H: Well, markers for a selection of the different moments involved in getting up here. You can see

they're all in different places. *Panda rhei* -
everything flows - like the river over there.

P: If we were actually to go back and look at one
again it would still say 'here and now', and it would
still be true. On the contrary, it demonstrates that
nothing changes at all. The only thing that changes
is our point of view, and that only because of an
illusion, as I told you before...

H: You said you had a proof?

P: Yes, although as I said, the proof is no longer
extant. The essence of it is that our true vision
would show, as Mr Blake will say, 'everything as it
is, infinite.' I saw this once, on my way home from
an unusually good party, when the goddess Dike
showed me reality in the blink of an eye, which for
me had no time. You can read about this in the
fragment of my poem that survives, called *The Way
of Truth*.

Act 3

(*The same*)

Heraclitus: This banana, for instance: does it not
travel through time in the same way that we do?

See: now it is an unpeeled banana, and now ... it is half peeled ... and now ... haha! I've eaten it, and throw the skin into the nettles, thus.

Parmenides (stares at Heraclitus's hand where a moment before the banana had been, puts an index finger to each temple, and wobbles slightly as if in a trance): I seem to see ... a banana extended in time, like a wavy yellow pole with a crescent shaped cross section ... half way up the pole expands as if into a flower ... but the flower is only the cross section of a now elaborate stem ... the flowerlike stem gets wider and more irregular but its central part gets smaller until, at the top, the stem disappears and the flower extends itself to one side suddenly, like a thin branch with crazy spiralling protrusions. Then the end of the branch disappears into a green tangle of insane complexity. It's ... oh, I've lost it. It's like one of those magic pictures. You lose the 3D if you move your head.

H: Ha! The banana in time. I suppose the green tangle is the nettles over there?

P: I think I lost my grip then. Even a clump of nettles can overwhelm the unprepared mind.

H: Perhaps you shouldn't drink retsina after Theakstons Old Peculiar?

P: Anyway, the point is, from the point of view of objective science, isn't a banana just how I've described it? At any rate, the small part of its history when you are eating it?

H: No doubt. And that being the case, we are like that too: spiralling wavy things with cloaks wrapping and unwrapping around us as we perform our dance of fate... . Isn't it strange how even when one is trying to describe a solid, like a sculpture, one finds oneself using the continuous present tense (the *-ing* words - spiralling, wrapping, unwrapping)? One describes a solid thing in a sequence, as though one were looking first at this part, then at another.

P: The continuous present... spiralling... using... looking... . But let's not get too mystical.

H: Perhaps at any rate we are approaching a solution to the problem of change, that is, how can change occur?

P: As I've always argued, change is impossible.

H: Explain?

P: Let us take object A. If it does not change, it remains object A, which is not problematical. But if it changes, it must perforce no longer be object A, but another object, which we might call B. Now clearly B is not A, because otherwise it would be A, which contradicts our hypothesis. Therefore if A changes, it follows that A ceases to exist. Therefore change is impossible.

H: That's exactly what the barman said when I paid for our drinks in the Dog and Duck with a silver drachma.

P: Yes. It's heartening to think that these obviously coarse people have philosophical souls.

H: Let us see if we can reach agreement on the problem of change.

P: Go ahead!

H: Take a banana (object A) to be, not the thing that was a banana and is now already partly a part (object B1) of the body of Heraclitus, and partly the beginning of a small compost heap (object B2), but the four dimensional yellow sculpture of your vision. Then indeed we can admit that a banana is unchanging. But what we call the banana is not object A nor objects B1 and B2, but the banana is the whole yellow wavy sculpture. The Time Banana. And we can agree that it is, from the point of view of your vision, unchanging. What we called object A (the banana before you ate it) is any cross section of the sculpture lower down in its main stem, and what we called objects B1 and B2 are other cross sections somewhere near the top.

P: I like it!

H: So change is a way of describing different parts of the same object, but the object is to be thought of as four dimensional. In other words, a thing is its whole self, including its entire fate in time.

P: Yes, it seems that way. But it follows then, that we never normally see a whole banana...

H: ...except after a suitable quantity of Theakstons Old Peculiar followed by the very best retsina!

P: Hmmm... perhaps this is off topic, or we may return to it another time, but it seems to me that the Time Banana may not be the same thing as what Plato will call, when he develops his theory of Forms, the Ideal Banana.

H: How so?

P: Because the Ideal Banana is the essence of banana in the mind of god, whereas the Time Banana is all the manifestations of the banana extended in time, which is more like the definition of the essence of banana that will be given by the godless existentialists in the 20th century. 'Existence precedes essence' and all that.

H: Perhaps if we take all the four dimensional bananas that ever have been and ever will be, a sort of Grand Unified Time Banana, that would be the Ideal Banana?

P: Maybe, but even so wouldn't the Grand Unified Time Banana be subject to chance events (albeit those chance events are foreordained)? Then the Grand Unified Time Banana would not be the Ideal banana.

H: Let us return to the matter in hand. We are tentatively agreed that... Oh look, there's someone... It's a woman, rather a fine looking one from this distance... Not a local: she's wearing a Greek peplos!

P: Oh yes, I see now! She's coming this way, waving her hands as though she's scattering something... no... it's a thread. She has a ball of twine in one hand and she's unwinding it in a trail behind her. And she has a chaplet of roses on her head: how charming! And a rustic shoulder bag with something in it.

H: See where she's laying the thread – very carefully right alongside my cheese-wrapper 'here and now' markers. She has the bound up hairstyle of a married woman. What a lovely neck! Such an irony that one can only see women's necks when they're already promised to someone else!

(They stand up, dusting crumbs off themselves)

P and H (in unison): Good day, revered lady.

Ariadne: Good day gentlemen!

H: Are you a nymph or goddess of these hills and woods? For otherwise, is it not strange that you should be seen out alone?

P (pushing in front of H and looking back at him): What a thing to say! (to Ariadne) Please forgive him for such a question! We can see that you are a respectable married woman. My friend here lives in constant awe of the shifting changes in everything, and sometimes it makes him forget ordinary etiquette.

Ariadne (laughing): Thank you for your consideration! But really, your friend is right: life is too short to spend much of it in mechanical pleasantries.

(H emerges from behind P)

Ariadne (points behind her): See where my thread stretches out down the hill: it is a little symbol of the shortness of my life. It begins where the youngest of the three Fates, Clotho, began to spin my story, and it stretches out as her older sister Lachesis makes me unwind it.

H: This most recent bit of your thread is right next to my little markers, that say 'here and now'.

A: Yes, the threads of our lives touch briefly, and all your little markers were true for me, too, as I passed each one.

H: So... you are a mortal?

A: I was mortal. You see, my thread had a beginning.

P: Was mortal? Who are you?

A: This is my ball of twine, with which my husband Theseus escaped from the labyrinth. But he forgot me on Naxos. Hero though he was, you might say he lost the thread.

H (aside to P): By the gods! It's Ariadne from the time of legends! (addressing Ariadne) So you are Ariadne? Didn't you marry a god afterwards? Did not the god also abandon you, and did you not hang yourself?

P: Heraclitus, have some respect! Do you not see you are addressing a goddess?

A: You are right, Parmenides. The hanging is but a dim memory of the way they used to hang me in a tree in effigy, so that I might survey the crops and see that all is fruitful. Like a corn dolly in England.

My husband is Dionysos, god of the vine. (She reaches inside her shoulder bag and brings out a bottle of wine)

H: Better not give any to him! He's had retsina on top of a couple of pints of Theakstons already!

A: You were discussing something as I came up the hill?

P: Indeed, madam, we were discussing how, seen rightly, everything is infinite and nothing changes, including bananas...

H: Yet it looks to me as though, as I like to say, 'nothing endures except change.' It is like your thread: you hold the whole of it in your hand. Somewhere in the middle of the ball is the other end, cut by the third weird sister, the oldest Fate Atropos, somewhen or nowhen, the end of your mortal life. As you walk through life, at each moment a different piece of the thread passes through your fingers...

P: That is what we call 'now', yet all the time the whole thread is there, just as the sisters have made it.

H: How is it, if the world and everything in it is one enormous tangle of all the threads the sisters have made, forever the same, how is it, if there is no movement (as Parmenides says) in this great space-time sculpture that is the universe, how is it that things always seem to change? How do your fingers seem to travel along the thread as you unwind your twine?

A: Perhaps they don't travel. Perhaps, as a mortal, one sees only a small part of reality. Then, one can see backwards a little way too, and that gives the feeling of memory, and the illusion of movement into the future. But we never see the future, do we? Perhaps only this, now, is real, as Parmenides says, and all movement is an illusion.

H: But if we seem to see change, does this not mean that at least our awareness changes?

A: Perhaps it does. But look! There is the thread of my old thoughts, stretching down the hill there. Was I aware when I passed the first of your little markers, or the second, or the third? I would say I was. So was not, is not my awareness always there, unchanging like my fate?

H: Yet only this last marker is close enough to read: 'here and now'. I am not as I was when I put the first marker in. You see, the Banana in Time has no sense of 'here and now' - it is stretched out over any number of 'theres and thens', and 'now' means nothing to it. But to me, only this marker is true, and to you, only that bit of thread, between your fingers, now.

P (holds out his cup): Perhaps another retsina would help?

H (sternly): I don't think so.

A (pouring from her bottle): It's all right, Heraclitus. This wine is from the god.

H: Will it change us?

A: Yes. It is the wine of astonishment. Its vintage is now.

P: May I ask you something?

A: Of course!

P: If you are no longer mortal, how can the thread of your life have an end?

A: Because I am not going in the direction of the thread. I am going *up*. I can go *up* from any point of the thread. My thread has ends, but my existence has no end: do you see?

(P and H look at each other in puzzlement, and shrug)

P: We see this awesome view, and the flowers in your hair, and the river below...

H: ...flowing constantly...

P: ...yet ever the same...

P and H together: ...proving us both right...

A: Is not the wine good?

Milton Marmalade's twenty answers

Here are the answers. The questions are in a parallel universe, so you'll have to make them up yourself.

1. Yes, in a way. But then again, no. Vanilla with ginger bits please. (I was once accused of being vanilla. But I'm proud of being vanilla. But I also like the ginger bits.)

2. Yes, you are quite right. Although there is very little you can say that isn't true in some sort of way. It follows of course that the contrary must also usually be true as well. This is because there is no strict connection between language and reality, a fact frequently exploited by politicians and other dubious sales people.

3. I try to compare thinking with reality. Sometimes I'm wrong. But then, as the Beatles said, 'when I'm wrong I'm right, where I belong I'm right, dum dum dum... [...] I'm fixing a hole where the rain gets in [&c.].'

4. No, only on alternate Wednesdays and only then if the moon is gibbous, otherwise I stick to cappuccino made in a proper espresso machine with Fairtrade arabica coffee beans freshly ground. I usually add amaretto syrup, one Imperial teaspoon.

5. I know it's deeply unfashionable to say you like the Beatles, but does that mean that all those people who bought their records were wrong? 'Picture yourself on a boat on a river, with tangerine trees and marmalade skies...' Marmalade. See?

6. Yes, I think most people do. A doctor once told me that studies have shown that 97% of people do and 3% are liars. Don't get involved in the wrong struggles. We are what we are. As long as being what we are harms no-one, what's the problem?

7. I am working in a shed at the back of the Co-op in Milton Keynes. This is because I need isolation to complete my master works, and frankly no-one is going to bother me there.

8. You see, when Myfanwy is not here then at first I feel a great sense of freedom. I am a man in a shed and I can do whatever I like (within the limits of the shed). But then after a while I get restless and have to go out, and I start prowling around looking for upmarket chocolate. That is not a euphemism for anything, I mean upmarket chocolate. 75% or so with chilli or ginger bits in it. Then I get melancholy but I console myself with the thought that melancholy is poetic. I might attempt a poem. I think chthonic is a good word but then I think it is pretentious and no-one will understand it and actually a good writer should write for the heart, so

I cross it out. After a while I re-read the poem and realise it's rubbish and find myself thinking how nice it would be if Myfanwy were to be making me a cup of tea right now, in the shed. Which might be a euphemism or it might be just for the companionship and tea. Or it might be a euphemism.

9. Reality is what is left when we stop thinking.

10. Do not trust anything you see written down. There is usually some salient fact left out which would change everything.

11. Only the heart knows the truth.

12. I used to have a lot of theories about life, the universe and everything. I wish I'd written them down, because if I could remember what they were I suspect I'd find them all correct and also realise that at the time I never understood them.

13. 'There's nothing you can do that can't be done...'

14. There are two kinds of soulmate. The ideal ones who represent the mirror of your soul, and with whom you fall achingly in love, and the real ones. The real ones are wonderful, but in a more ordinary way, which is suitable, because we too are ordinary.

15. 'Let it be, let it be, let it be yeah let it be, whisper words of wisdom, let it be.'

16. Bach.

17. Books! I sometimes give away books to create more shelf space so that I don't have to double-shelf them. Later I realise that the answer to a particular question was in the book I gave away.

18. I once believed the answer would be found in a book. That's why I have so many of them. My father had quantities of books, ostensibly for the same reason. One day I bought him a book with the answer on the first page. I don't think he ever read it. I had to move all his books, and the answer was somewhere in most of them. Probably he had read the answer many times.

19. Reading is not the same as understanding. Reading is not the same as doing. Doing and understanding are linked.

20. Love is all you need. But how?

Further reading for curly minds

If you have enjoyed this book you will probably also enjoy Milton Marmalade's novel *A Mermaid in the Bath*, available from bookstores and on Amazon worldwide.

Go to www.MiltonMarmalade.uk for the random thoughts of Milton Marmalade and a sample of the book.

www.ingramcontent.com/pod-product-compliance
Lightning Source LLC
Chambersburg PA
CBHW030600130626
46552CB00006B/2616